Dear Parent:
Your child's love of reading

anythink

Every child learns to read in a different way speed. Some go back and forth between rea favorite books again and again. Others read through each level in order. You can help your young reader improve and become more confident by encouraging his or her own interests and abilities. From books your child reads with you to the first books he or she reads alone, there are I Can Read Books for every stage of reading:

SHARED READING
Basic language, word repetition, and whimsical illustrations, ideal for sharing with your emergent reader

BEGINNING READING
Short sentences, familiar words, and simple concepts for children eager to read on their own

READING WITH HELP
Engaging stories, longer sentences, and language play for developing readers

READING ALONE
Complex plots, challenging vocabulary, and high-interest topics for the independent reader

ADVANCED READING
Short paragraphs, chapters, and exciting themes for the perfect bridge to chapter books

I Can Read Books have introduced children to the joy of reading since 1957. Featuring award-winning authors and illustrators and a fabulous cast of beloved characters, I Can Read Books set the standard for beginning readers.

A lifetime of discovery begins with the magical words "I Can Read!"

Visit www.icanread.com for information
on enriching your child's reading experience.

Mouse Tales

BY ARNOLD LOBEL

HarperCollinsPublishers

HarperCollins®, 🔖®, and I Can Read Book® are trademarks of HarperCollins Publishers.

Library of Congress Catalog Card Number: 72-76511
ISBN-10: 0-06-023941-7 (trade bdg.) — ISBN-13: 978-0-06-023941-1 (trade bdg.)
ISBN-10: 0-06-023942-5 (lib. bdg.) — ISBN-13: 978-0-06-023942-8 (lib. bdg.)
ISBN-10: 0-06-444013-3 (pbk.) — ISBN-13: 978-0-06-444013-4 (pbk.)

16 17 18 SCP 20 19
❖

CONTENTS

"Papa, we are all
in bed now,"
said the mouse boys.
"Please tell us a tale."
"I will do better than that,"
said Papa.
"I will tell you seven tales—
one for each of you—
if you promise
to go right to sleep
when I am done."
"Oh yes, we will,"
said the boys.

And Papa began . . .

THE WISHING WELL

A mouse once found

a wishing well.

"Now all of my wishes

can come true!"

she cried.

She threw a penny

into the well

and made a wish.

"OUCH!"

said the wishing well.

The next day the mouse

came back to the well.

She threw a penny

into the well

and made a wish.

"OUCH!" said the well.

The next day

the mouse came back again.

She threw a penny

into the well.

"I wish this well

would not say ouch," she said.

"OUCH!" said the well.

"That hurts!"

"What shall I do?"

cried the mouse.

"My wishes

will never ever

come true this way!"

The mouse ran home.

She took the pillow

from her bed.

"This may help,"

said the mouse,

and she ran back

to the well.

The mouse threw the pillow

into the well.

Then she threw

a penny into the well

and made a wish.

"Ah. That feels

much better!"

said the well.

"Good!" said the mouse.

"Now I can start wishing."

After that day

the mouse made many wishes

by the well.

And every one of them

came true.

CLOUDS

A little mouse went for a walk
with his mother.
They went to the top of a hill
and looked at the sky.

"Look!" said Mother. "We can see
pictures in the clouds."
The little mouse and his mother
saw many pictures in the clouds.
They saw a castle . . .

a rabbit . . .

a mouse.

"I am going to pick flowers,"
said Mother.

"I will stay here
and watch the clouds,"
said the little mouse.

The little mouse

saw a big cloud in the sky.

It grew bigger and bigger.

The cloud became a cat.

The cat came nearer and nearer

to the little mouse.

"Help!" shouted the little mouse,

and he ran to his mother.

"There is a big cat in the sky!"
cried the little mouse.
"I am afraid!"
Mother looked up at the sky.
"Do not be afraid," she said.
"See, the cat has turned back
into a cloud again."

The little mouse

saw that this was true,

and he felt better.

He helped his mother pick flowers,

but he did not look up at the sky

for the rest of the afternoon.

VERY TALL MOUSE
AND VERY SHORT MOUSE

Once there was a very tall mouse
and a very short mouse
who were good friends.

When they met
Very Tall Mouse would say,
"Hello, Very Short Mouse."
And Very Short Mouse would say,
"Hello, Very Tall Mouse."

The two friends would often

take walks together.

As they walked along

Very Tall Mouse would say,

"Hello birds."

And Very Short Mouse would say,

"Hello bugs."

When they
passed by a garden
Very Tall Mouse would say,
"Hello flowers."
And Very Short Mouse
would say,
"Hello roots."

When they passed by a house

Very Tall Mouse would say,

"Hello roof."

And Very Short Mouse

would say,

"Hello cellar."

One day the two mice

were caught in a storm.

Very Tall Mouse said,

"Hello raindrops."

And Very Short Mouse said,

"Hello puddles."

They ran indoors to get dry.

"Hello ceiling,"

said Very Tall Mouse.

"Hello floor,"

said Very Short Mouse.

Soon the storm was over.

The two friends

ran to the window.

Very Tall Mouse held
Very Short Mouse up to see.

"Hello rainbow!"
they both said together.

THE MOUSE AND THE WINDS

A mouse went out in his boat,

but there was no wind.

The boat did not move.

"Wind!" shouted the mouse.

"Come down and blow my boat

across the lake!"

"Here I am," said the west wind.

The west wind blew and blew.

The mouse and the boat

went up in the air . . .

and landed

on the roof of a house.

"Wind!" shouted the mouse.

"Come down and blow my boat

off this house!"

"Here I am," said the east wind.

The east wind blew and blew.

The mouse and the boat

and the house

went up in the air . . .

and landed on the top of a tree.

"Wind!" shouted the mouse.

"Come down and blow my boat

off this house

and off this tree!"

"Here I am,"
said the south wind.
The south wind blew and blew.
The mouse and the boat
and the house and the tree
went up in the air . . .

and landed

on the top of a mountain.

"Wind!" shouted the mouse.

"Come down and blow my boat

off this house

and off this tree

and off this mountain!"

"Here I am," said the north wind.

The north wind blew and blew.

The mouse and the boat

and the house and the tree

and the mountain

went up in the air . . .

and came down into the lake.

The mountain sank
and became an island.

The tree landed on the island
and burst into bloom.

The house landed next to the tree.

A lady looked out of a window

in the house

and said,

"What a nice place to live!"

And the mouse just sailed away.

THE JOURNEY

There was a mouse

who wanted to visit

his mother.

So he bought a car

and started to drive

to his mother's house.

He drove  and

drove  and drove

until the car fell apart.

But at the side of the road

there was a person

selling roller skates.

So the mouse bought

two roller skates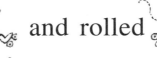

and put them on.

He rolled and rolled

and rolled

until the wheels fell off.

But at the side of the road

there was a person

who was selling boots.

So the mouse bought

two boots and put them on.

He tramped and tramped

 and tramped

until there were

big holes in the boots.

But at the side of the road

there was a person

who was selling sneakers.

So the mouse bought

two sneakers.

He put them on and ran

and ran  and ran

until the sneakers

were all worn out.

So he took the sneakers off

and walked and

walked and walked

until his feet hurt so much

that he could not go on.

But at the side of the road

there was a person

who was selling feet.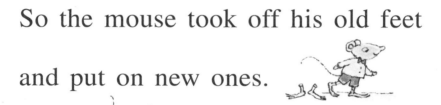

So the mouse took off his old feet

and put on new ones.

He ran the rest of the way

to his mother's house.

When he got there

his mother was glad to see him.

She hugged him  and

kissed him,

and she said, "Hello, my son.

You are looking fine—

and what nice new feet

you have!"

THE OLD MOUSE

There was an old mouse

who went for a walk every day.

The old mouse

did not like children.

When he saw them on the street

he would shout,

"Go away, horrid things!"

One day the old mouse

was taking his walk.

All at once, his suspenders broke,

and his pants fell down.

Some ladies came by.

"Help, help!" cried the old mouse.

But the ladies screamed,

"Your pants have fallen down!"

And they ran away.

The old mouse ran home
and cried, "Help me!"
But his wife only said,
"You look silly
in your underwear,"
and gave him a hit on the head.

The old mouse began to cry.

Some children passed by.

"Poor old mouse," they said,

"we will help you.

Here is some chewing gum.

It will hold your pants up

very well."

"Look!" cried the old mouse.

"My pants are up!

This chewing gum is great.

These pants will never

fall down again!"

Those pants never did
fall down again.
And after that, the old mouse
was always kind to children
when he went for his walk.

THE BATH

There was once a mouse

who was dirty,

so he took a bath.

The water

filled up the bathtub.

But the mouse was still dirty,

so he let the water

run over onto the floor.

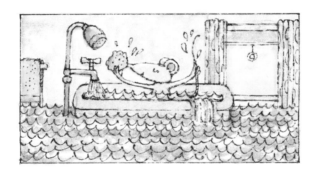

The water

filled up the bathroom.

But the mouse was still dirty,

so he let the water

run out of the window.

The water

filled up the street.

But the mouse was still dirty,

so he let the water
run into the house
next door.

The people
in the house next door
cried, "Turn off the water!
We have had
our bath today!"

But the mouse was still dirty,
so he let the water
run all over the whole town.

The people in the town cried,
"Turn off the water!
You are very clean now!"

The mouse said,

"Yes, you are right.

I am clean now."

So he turned off the water.

By then

the town was all wet.

But the mouse
did not care.

He rubbed himself
with a big towel
until he was very dry.

And then
he went right to sleep.

"Is anybody awake?"
asked Papa.

There was no answer.

Seven small mice

were snoring.

"Good night, my boys,"

said Papa,

"and sleep well.

I will see you all

in the morning."

The End